Aesop's Fables

All-time Favourite Stories

An imprint of Om Books International

Reprinted in 2016 by

An imprint of Om Books International

Corporate & Editorial Office
A 12, Sector 64, Noida 201 301
Uttar Pradesh, India
Phone: +91 120 477 4100
Email: editorial@ombooks.com
Website: www.ombooksinternational.com

Sales Office
107, Darya Ganj, New Delhi 110 002, India
Phone: +91 11 4000 9000
Fax: +91 11 2327 8091
Email: sales@ombooks.com
Website: www.ombooks.com

Content: Subhojit Sanyal
Illustration: Salil Anand, Kushiram, Jyoti

ISBN : 978 93 81607 27 5

Printed in India

10 9 8 7 6 5 4

Contents

The Fox and the Grapes

One day, a fox was walking around in the forest. He was very hungry and was desperately looking for something to eat.

Suddenly, he spotted a bunch of juicy grapes hanging from a tree, a little ahead. The fox rushed to the tree and looked at the grapes closely. "These grapes are so plump, it seems that the juice will start pouring out of them right now!" thought the fox to himself.

The only problem was that the grapes were on
a branch, which was very high from the ground.
The fox tried to jump and grab the bunch of
grapes, but he came nowhere near it.

The fox's mouth was watering at the thought of gobbling the grapes! So he decided to try even harder to get the grapes. He walked away from the tree a little bit and then came running towards it. As he came near the tree, he jumped very high, but even then not a single grape could he reach.

This continued for quite some time. The fox kept running towards the tree, he jumped higher and higher, but he came no closer to plucking the grapes.

Finally, when he became very tired with all the running and jumping, the fox said, "O, these grapes are sour most certainly! Why am I wasting my time on them?" The fox walked away from the tree, his tongue hanging from his tired mouth. But insulting what he could not get, did not make him feel any better!

The Tortoise and the Ducks

The lazy tortoise had been punished. He had been too lazy to leave his house and come to Lord Jupiter's wedding. And so, the mighty Jupiter cursed him, and he always had to carry his house on his back. Now, however much he tried, he just could not rid himself of the heavy load of his house.

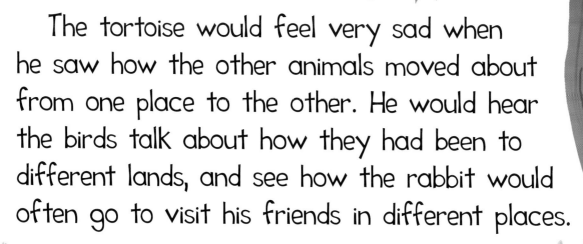

The tortoise would feel very sad when he saw how the other animals moved about from one place to the other. He would hear the birds talk about how they had been to different lands, and see how the rabbit would often go to visit his friends in different places.

He too wanted to see the world, but alas, he could not even move a little bit without making a lot of effort.

One day, he spoke of his woes to two ducks. The ducks too were very sad on hearing of the tortoise's dreams and decided to help him.

"We can help you, but you will have to be absolutely silent during the whole journey. Do you think you can do that?"

The tortoise was more than willing to be quiet, if that is what it took to travel around the world.

The ducks then took a long stick and asked the tortoise to hold on to it with his teeth. Then, the two ducks grabbed the two ends of the stick with their feet and started to fly.

The tortoise was extremely happy when he saw the land below him grow smaller and smaller, as he soon reached the clouds. He was indeed overjoyed.

The tall trees looked
like the smallest shrubs
to him, so high was he! The
forest looked like nothing more
than a patch of grass and the
lake looked like a tiny puddle.

Just then, a crow flew past them. The crow was amazed to see the sight of a flying tortoise and said, "Goodness me! You really must be the King of tortoises!"

The tortoise felt very proud on hearing the crow's words. He began, "Why ye..." But just as he opened his mouth, he lost his grip on the stick, and even before he could realize what had happened, he hit the ground below. And that was the end of the foolish tortoise! Pride always leads to fall.

The Dog, the Cock and the Fox

The dog and the cock were the best of friends. One day, the two of them decided that they needed to travel and see the world. So the two of them set off and made their way to the woods.

They travelled a long distance, before they reached the forest. It was very late in the day and the Sun was almost about to set. The cock told the dog, "We better find a place to stay for the night. We can start off on our travels through the forest again tomorrow morning." The dog readily agreed.

A little distance ahead, they saw a tree with a hollow in its trunk. The dog turned to his friend and said, "This will be the best place for us to spend the night. You can go up and sleep on one of those branches, while I can rest in the hollow."

The fox, who was sleeping nearby, awoke on hearing the the voices. He looked around and spotted the cock sitting on the tree. The fox was now very happy. "Ah! Tomorrow morning I can get myself a good breakfast!" he said to himself.

The two friends bid each other a good night and before long, they were both fast asleep.

As the Sun's rays fell on the cock's eyes in the morning, out of habit he yelled, "Cock-a-doodle-doooooo!"

Very slowly, the fox walked up to the cock and said, "Hello there, my friend! Welcome to the forest! Why don't you come down from that branch and I can then show you around the wild..."

The cock was no fool. He knew that the minute he would come down, the fox would pounce on him and eat him up. He decided to teach the fox a lesson.

"Thank you for your generous offer, kind Sir! Why don't you come up here to me instead and you can tell me a little more about the forest. Please come in through the hollow in the trunk, it will be easier for you to get up here!"

The fox was delighted. The cock was making it very easy for him. Without wasting another second, the fox ran around to the hollow. Little did he know that the dog was sitting there, waiting for him to enter!

The fox got such a severe beating from the dog, that he decided never to trick anyone again. Those who try to cheat get cheated themselves.

The Thirsty Crow

The poor crow had been flying for a long, long time. He had gone to the village to meet one of his relatives and was now flying back to his house in the city.

It was a very hot day, and the distance between the village and the city was rather long too. The crow had not taken any break in between and had just kept flying, because he wanted to get back to the city before dark.

But the crow was very thirsty. He really needed a drink of cool water. He kept looking around him, trying to find a pond, or a river, or any place where he could drink some water from.

Finally, as he was about to reach his nest, he saw a rather large jug kept outside a house. The crow flew down towards the jug at once, hoping to find some water there.

Lo and behold, it was water! The crow was overjoyed and he pushed his beak into the jug at once. But it was pointless! The water in the jug was very little, and the mouth of the jug was so narrow that the crow could not put his head very deep inside.

"Oh my, what bad luck! Even when I do find water, I cannot drink any of it. Why does everything always happen to me?" cried the crow.

But then he told himself, "I should find a solution to this problem instead of crying like a baby!" And then the crow hit upon an idea.

He found some small pebbles right next to the jug, and picking up one pebble at a time, he started throwing them into the jug.

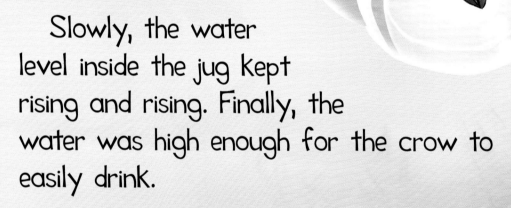

Slowly, the water level inside the jug kept rising and rising. Finally, the water was high enough for the crow to easily drink.

After quenching his thirst, the happy crow took off and flew straight to his house. And so, from the crow we learn that we should try and try until we succeed.

The Donkey and the Salt

Freddie, the salt merchant, was in a fix. The shop from the other side of the river had asked him to come and deliver his salt to them. They had even said that they wanted him to sell them his salt every week. This would mean a lot of money for Freddie.

But there was just one problem. He would have to carry the salt to the shop and even cross the river in the process. Naturally, Freddie realized that he could not lift the heavy bags of salt all by himself and so, Freddie went and bought himself a donkey.

Next morning, Freddie loaded two huge bags of salt on his donkey and set off towards the shop on the other side of the river.

Now, Freddie's donkey was having a very tough time. After all, the two bags of salt that were hanging on his back were extremely heavy. He could barely gather enough strength to stand!

But there was nothing that he could do. So he kept walking, very slowly, and soon they were at the river. Freddie urged his donkey forward and they started to cross the river.

The stones at the bed of the river were very slippery and it was getting more and more difficult for the donkey to walk with that heavy load on his back.

Just as they reached the middle of the river, the donkey's foot slipped on one of the rocks and he fell down. What happened next was a big surprise for the donkey. A lot of the salt got dissolved in the water!

As soon as the donkey got up, he realized that the load on his back was much lighter. The salt had flown away with the river and now he only had to carry a light load to the shop. It was then that the donkey had an idea!

Ever since, every time that Freddie had to go to the shop to deliver his salt, the donkey would deliberately slip while crossing the river and thereby, lighten his load.

This went on for quite some days and finally, Freddie understood what his donkey was up to. So he decided to teach the animal a lesson.

The next day, Freddie had to go to the shop once again to deliver his salt. He put two bags on his donkey's back and together, they started travelling to the river.

Just as they reached the river, the donkey decided to fall and lighten his load. But alas, this time the result was different! Freddie had filled the bags with sponges. So when the donkey actually fell into the water, instead of dissolving, the sponges just became ten times heavier than they were.

The donkey did not know what to do, and had to walk the rest of the distance with a very, very heavy load on his back. He was trying to cheat his master and he had to pay the price for it.

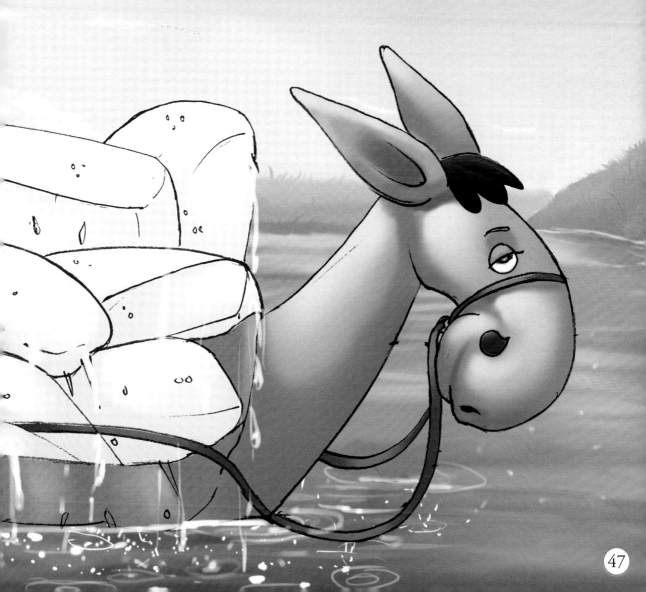

The Two Goats

Daisy the goat decided to go for a little stroll. There was a cool breeze blowing and it was the perfect weather to go for a walk. She kept walking for quite some time, stopping to eat the green grass that grew on the side of the hill and soon she reached the edge of the hill.

Daisy was about to go back, when she chanced to look ahead at the hillside in front of her. She saw the greenest grass that she had ever seen in her lifetime, growing right across from where she stood. And there was a lot of it!

Daisy knew that she just had to cross the long log that connected the two hills and eat to her heart's content. The thought of all that green grass made her mouth water and she could wait no longer.

But just as she kept her foot on the log, she saw another goat come from the hill in front and also step on to the log. Daisy was a little surprised at first. After all, there was just enough space on the log for one of them to cross through it, one at a time.

She was sure that the other goat too could understand that, but even then, the other goat was not stepping back to let Daisy cross first.

"That goat is so mean, she just won't let me cross first, even though I was the first person on this log bridge! Hmph! What does she think of herself? Even I won't let her go first..." thought Daisy, and started moving forward.

Very slowly, Daisy kept balancing herself and walking forward on the log bridge. The other goat too was walking forward and very soon, the two of them were face to face, right at the middle of the bridge.

"Listen here, I was on the bridge first. You should move back and let me cross over first!" demanded Daisy before the other goat.

But the other goat replied, "You saw me coming, you should have moved back yourself. Why should I go back all the way now? You go back and let me get to the other side!"

The two kept arguing like this for quite some time, but they were nowhere close to reaching a solution. After fighting, as to who would turn back, the two goats started clashing their horns against each other.

As soon as they started pushing each other, both goats lost their balance on the narrow log and fell straight down to the valley below. And that was no good for them, was it? It is better to yield than get hurt in a silly fight.

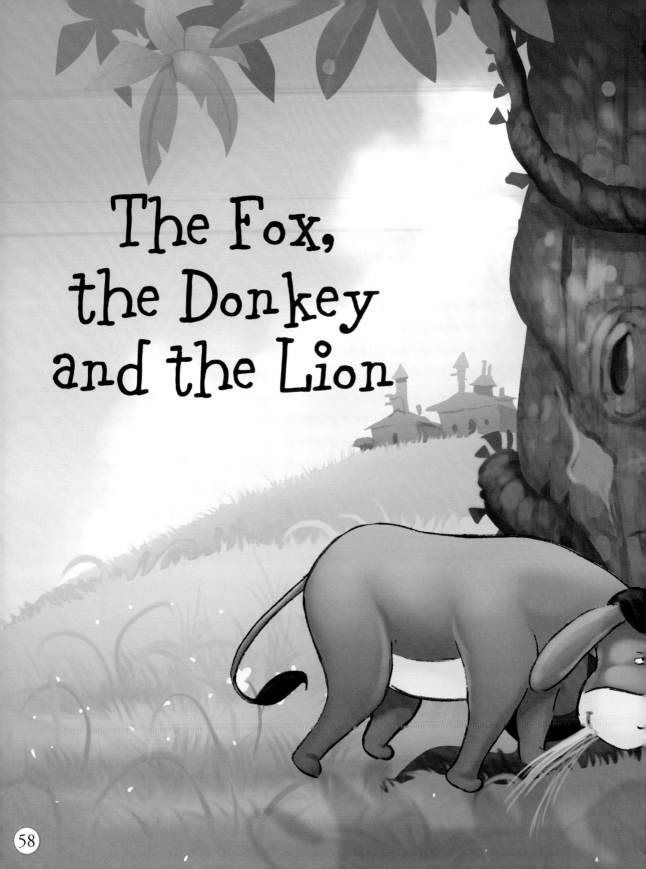

The Fox,
the Donkey
and the Lion

The donkey and the fox had recently become the best of friends. They would play with each other the whole day, and would also take long trips together in search of food.

While the donkey would be happy
eating some grass, the fox would
look for his own food, and together,
the two friends would sit down and
eat to their hearts' content.

One day, the donkey and the fox were walking in the forest, looking for some food, when they suddenly came across a lion.

The donkey naturally was very scared, and he started to cry. "Boo hooo hoooo hooooooo! The lion is going to eat me up! Oh I am so scared right now..."

The fox turned to him and said, "Oh stop crying, my friend! Don't worry, I will talk to the lion and take care of the matter. You just stop acting so silly!"

So saying, the fox walked over to the lion and in a very soft voice, so that the donkey could not hear anything, said, "My lord, I know that you are hungry and you are looking for your lunch. I suggest you take my friend, the 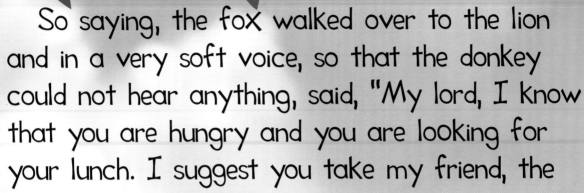 donkey to a pit quite close from here. Once you push him down there, you can take your time and eat him very easily!"

The lion was very pleased with the fox's offer and agreed to go along with them. The fox ran back to the donkey and said, "My friend, the lion has agreed to spare us. All we have to do is go and sit in that pit over there. The lion says that we will be safe over there!"

The donkey was naturally very pleased to hear that and he followed the fox to the pit at once. But as soon as they reached there, the fox cleverly pushed the donkey into the pit and then turned to the lion, saying, "Sire, your lunch is ready!"

What happened next was something that took the fox completely by surprise. Instead of going after the donkey, the lion jumped on the fox and beat him up. The fox could not even move.

The lion then helped pull the donkey out of the pit and said, "You can go, my friend! I will eat the fox for lunch, today."

The donkey was very grateful to the lion and he ran off from there immediately. Now the fox knew that if you do bad things to others, something bad will happen to you.

The Boy Who Cried "Wolf"

Joel the shepherd was very bored with his life. There was nothing exciting happening around him and he had to spend every day in the meadow, grazing his flock of sheep.

One day, just to have some fun with the people in the village, Joel started screaming, "Wolf, wolf!"

On hearing Joel's cries for help, several villagers rushed out of their houses with their sticks, and came to help Joel get rid of the wolf.

But as soon as they reached Joel, he started laughing. "What happened? Where is the wolf? Why are you laughing?" asked the worried villagers.

"I was just fooling you all," replied
Joel, still unable to control his laughter.
"There is no wolf anywhere. I just
wanted to have some fun."
Grumbling, the villagers
returned to their homes.

The next day, as Joel was coming back from the countryside with his sheep and was just about to enter the village, he decided to play the same prank on the villagers again.

"Help, help! This time there really is a wolf, it is attacking my sheep. Please help!" he cried once again. The villagers heard Joel screaming and thinking that he was speaking the truth this time, they once again came running out to help him.

But as they approached Joel, the young shepherd started laughing once again. The villagers were very angry this time. It had been twice that Joel had lied to them. The villagers cursed Joel and went back to their homes.

Joel decided to pull the prank once again the next day. Just as he reached the village, he started screaming "Wolf, Wolf" once again.

But even though the villagers heard him, this time they refused to do anything about it. They knew that Joel was surely lying again, and therefore, they did not bother coming out to help him.

Joel too realized that perhaps the villagers were wise to his joke now and decided to go back home with his flock. But just as he turned around, he saw that a wolf was really running towards his sheep.

Joel was extremely scared and started screaming, "Help, help! Please help me, this time there really is a wolf here! Oh please come, this is not a joke. My sheep will be killed!"

But no one came. No one believed Joel anymore. They were sure that Joel was just lying again to get them to come out.

Joel could not do anything about the wolf attacking his sheep. And so he learnt that liars are not believed, even when they speak the truth.